LAURENCE ANHOLT was born in London and brought up
mainly in Holland. His books have won numerous awards including
the Nestlé Smarties Gold Award for *Chimp and Zee*, the first story about
two lovable twin monkeys which he created in collaboration with his wife,
Catherine Anholt. Among his previous books for Frances Lincoln are
Can You Guess?, *Chimp and Zee*, *Chimp and Zee and the Big Storm*,
Monkey About with Chimp and Zee, *Chimp and Zee's Noisy Book*
(all illustrated by Catherine Anholt) and his Anholt's Artists series:
Camille and the Sunflowers, *Degas and the Little Dancer*,
Picasso and the Girl with a Ponytail, *Leonardo and the Flying Boy*
and *The Magical Garden of Claude Monet*.
Laurence lives with his family in a rambling farmhouse
near Lyme Regis in Dorset.

For my son, Tom – anything is possible

In memory of Lucy Keeling

Leonardo and the Flying Boy copyright © Frances Lincoln Limited 2000
Text and illustrations copyright © Laurence Anholt 2000

First published in Great Britain in 2000 by
Frances Lincoln Limited, 4 Torriano Mews,
Torriano Avenue, London NW5 2RZ

www.franceslincoln.com

This edition first published in 2003

British Library Cataloguing in Publication Data available on request

ISBN 0-7112-2132-4

Printed in China
9 8 7 6 5 4

Visit the Anholt website at **www.anholt.co.uk**

PHOTOGRAPHIC ACKNOWLEDGMENTS

Please note: the pages in this book are not numbered. The story begins on page 4.

Paintings and drawings by Leonardo da Vinci (1452–1519)
Front cover, Pages 3, 34 & 35: *Birds' Flight* (detail), Codex on the Flight of Birds, Folio 8r, Biblioteca Reale, Turin.
Photograph Scala, Florence
Page 2: *Notes on astronomical studies* (detail), Codex Leicester. Photograph AKG London
Page 7 (above left): *The infant and womb* (detail), RL 19102r. The Royal Collection © 2000 Her Majesty Queen Elizabeth II
Page 7 (above right): *A Star of Bethlehem and other plants* (detail), RL 12424. The Royal Collection © 2000 Her Majesty
Queen Elizabeth II
Page 7 (below left): *The outer luminosity of the Moon* (detail), Codex Leicester, Folio 2r. Photograph Bridgeman Art
Library/Christie's Images
Page 7 (below right): *Test for the Wing of an 'Ornitottero'* (detail), Manuscript B, Folio 88v, Bibliothèque de l'Institut de France,
Paris. Photograph AKG London
Pages 14, 15 & 28: *Design for a flying machine* (details), Manuscript B, Folio 38v, Bibliothèque de l'Institut de France, Paris.
Photograph The Art Archive
Page 16: *Seven studies of Grotesque Faces* (details), Galleria dell'Accademia, Venice. Photograph Bridgeman Art Library
Page 20: *Portrait of Mona Lisa, called La Gioconda* (1503–1506), Louvre, Paris. Photograph AKG London/Erich Lessing
Page 33: *Portrait of Leonardo da Vinci*, Copy after (unattributed), RL 12726. The Royal Collection © 2000 Her Majesty
Queen Elizabeth II

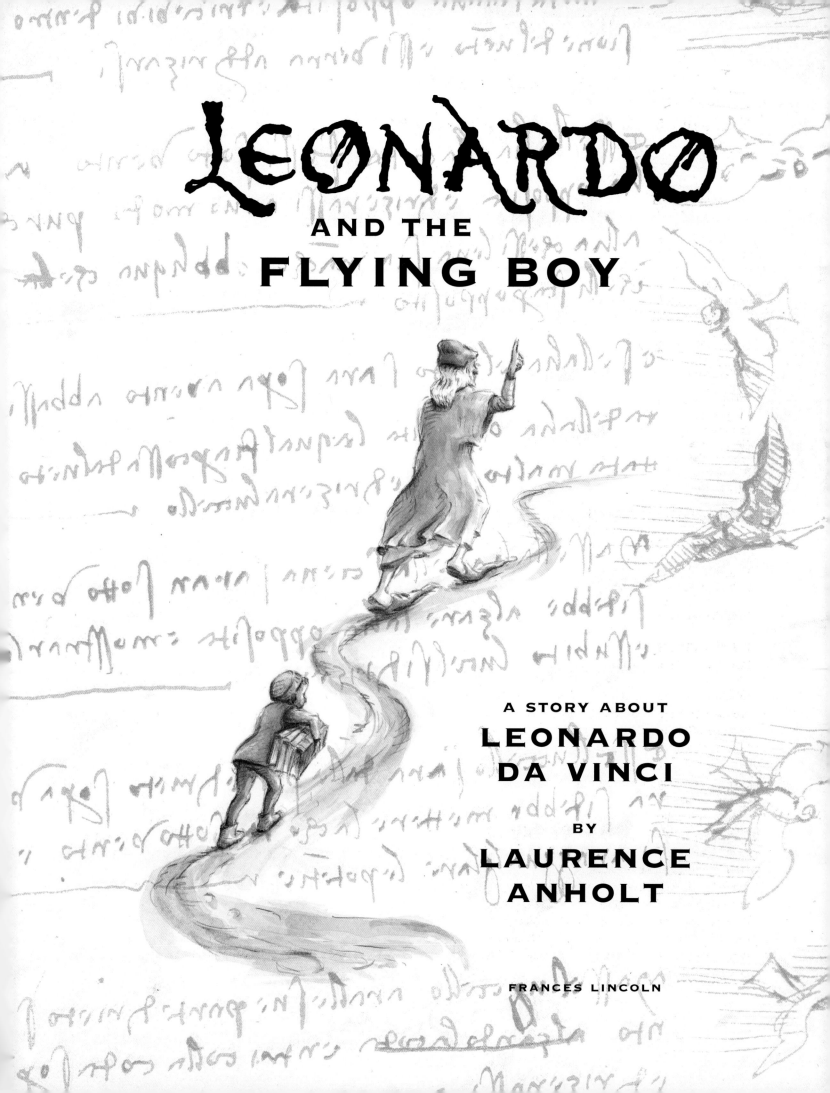

LEONARDO
AND THE
FLYING BOY

A STORY ABOUT
**LEONARDO
DA VINCI**

BY

**LAURENCE
ANHOLT**

FRANCES LINCOLN

THERE were no space ships
or aeroplanes when Zoro was a boy.
The sky belonged to the birds. But one
man dreamed of something incredible.
"One day, Zoro," he told his pupil,
"people will sail through the clouds
and look down at the world below.

Anything is possible."

The man with the
amazing dream and a beard like
a wizard was Leonardo da Vinci.

Anything seemed possible in Leonardo's busy studio. He was
a painter, a sculptor, a musician and a scientist.

Sometimes he showed Zoro his beautiful notebooks where
a thousand ideas spilled from every page.

"We must try to understand everything," said the great genius…

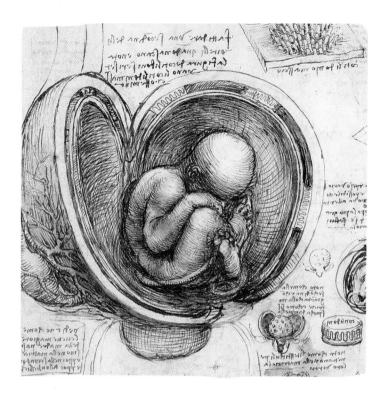

How does life begin?

How does a plant grow?

How do the planets move?

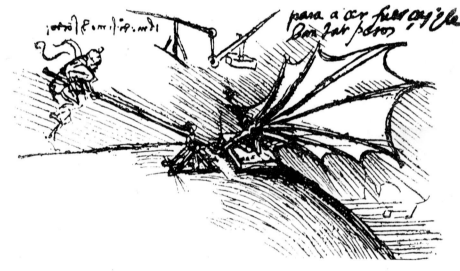

And how could a person fly like a bird?

But when Zoro tried to read the books, he found them written back to front:

ɿoɿɿim ɒ ni bɒɘɿ ɘd ʏlno bluoɔ ƨbɿow ɟɘɿɔɘƨ ɘɟʇ oƨ

There was one place where Zoro could never go –

one mysterious workshop where the door was always locked.

No one was allowed in there except Leonardo himself.

Zoro longed to know what was inside. 'Perhaps it's

a fantastic sculpture,' he thought, 'or a huge war machine.'

In the studio everyone had to work hard.

Zoro mixed colours, cleaned brushes and practised his drawings.

"When I am grown up, I will have my own studio,"

he said, "and a secret workshop too!"

"Of course you will, Zoro,"

smiled Leonardo.

Leonardo was a kind man. If ever he found an animal which was sick or hungry, he would bring it home for the pupils to look after.

But one day, Leonardo found something very strange.

He dragged the wild and noisy creature into the studio, where it kicked and fought and spat at the great artist.

"What is it?" asked Zoro.

"It's a boy!" laughed Leonardo. "A very wild boy. He's never been to school and his mother is too poor to look after him. She begged me to give him some work before he ends up in prison."

The wild boy grabbed Leonardo's hand and bit very hard. Leonardo pretended to be angry, but Zoro could see that he was laughing.

"I'll call you Salai," said Leonardo. "It means 'Little Devil', and that's exactly what you are."

So Salai came to stay in the studio and, although he was a bad boy, everyone grew fond of him.

"But you can't wear those rags," said Leonardo. "I'm going to buy you a real velvet suit and some shoes... Now where did I leave my purse?"

They searched high and low until at last Zoro found the money – hidden in Salai's filthy coat.

Zoro couldn't believe it.

Who would dare to steal

from Leonardo da Vinci?

Day after day, Leonardo dreamed up inventions
of every kind. Zoro was amazed to see...

a parachute,

the very first bicycle,

a deadly war machine,

a gadget for walking on water,

a life belt,

and a diving suit.

Once, he built a machine for
cutting and polishing
glass and made
himself a pair
of spectacles.

"Now I can keep
an eye on Salai!"
he said, winking at Zoro.

Early one morning, Leonardo took Zoro

into town to look for interesting faces to draw.

When he noticed someone especially beautiful

or unusually ugly, Leonardo would follow them,

making dozens of sketches.

They came to the market where a lady

was selling birds in tiny cages.

Leonardo looked at the birds, then,

to Zoro's surprise, he bought them all;

but instead of taking the birds home as pets,

Leonardo told Zoro to open the cages.

Everybody stared. No one could understand.

"A bird should be free," said Leonardo. "Look, Zoro! Can you see how their wings push against the air? It gives me an idea..."

Leonardo began to run.

As soon as he got home, he locked himself in the secret workshop again. Zoro could hear hammering and sawing from inside.

Hour after hour, Zoro waited, but Leonardo wouldn't stop for food or drink. What on earth was he building?

'It must be something incredible,' thought Zoro. 'Something no one has ever dreamed of.'

At last he fell asleep on the steps outside.

Leonardo began a wonderful painting of a woman called Mona Lisa. She had to sit for weeks without moving, so Leonardo paid acrobats and musicians to stop her getting bored.

Zoro stared at the dreamy green mountains and the twisting rivers. 'Surely no one has painted anything so perfect,' he thought.

The face in the painting was smiling – a mysterious, gentle smile.

'It's as if she knows some secret,' thought Zoro. 'As if she has seen inside that locked room.'

Suddenly Salai crept up behind him.

"Come with me, Zoro!" he hissed. "I'll show you something more interesting than that picture." Salai looked very guilty. He dragged Zoro out of the studio and quietly down the stairs. At the door of the secret workshop, Salai pulled out a big bunch of keys.

"You stole them!" gasped Zoro. "Leonardo will throw you back on the street!"

Salai only laughed and unlocked the door.

Zoro knew he shouldn't be there. He should turn and run to Leonardo, but... he just had to see inside that secret room.

Zoro couldn't believe his eyes!

An extraordinary machine filled the room.

Its wings were like a great eagle.

"Help me pull it outside," ordered Salai.

"If we wait until Leonardo is ready,

we will never fly. Anyway you are the only

one small enough to fit in the machine.

It was made for you –

you will be the Flying Boy!"

"Leonardo will be furious," whispered Zoro.

"Not when he sees you flying above the studio!" shouted Salai. "Come on, Zoro. Help me."

So, as Leonardo worked upstairs, Salai and Zoro hauled and dragged the heavy machine out of the workshop, along the streets and far into the fields.

Salai pointed to the highest hill.

"We will try the machine from there," he said.

As the sun set,

they reached the top.

"Now," panted Salai,

"just lie in here. When you pedal,

the wings will flap."

Zoro was shaking. He felt ill.

"Perhaps the machine isn't finished,"

he cried. "We should be patient…"

But Salai was already strapping

Zoro into the machine and dragging

it towards the edge of the hill.

Zoro was terrified. He began to shout.

Suddenly there was a gust of wind,

Salai pushed and the flying machine

left the ground.

Zoro looked down at the world below;

he was sobbing with fear,

but for a few seconds…

...he flew like a bird!

"It works! It works!" shouted the wild
boy far below.

But something was wrong!
The bird was too heavy. Zoro pedalled
and pulled, but the machine began to fall.

At that moment, Leonardo came
running across the fields. Zoro tugged
on the ropes and screamed, as the machine
fell like a stone and crashed into a tree.

Leonardo himself pulled Zoro's limp body
from the wrecked machine and carefully
carried him home.

Salai followed slowly –
his head hanging in shame.

Zoro was lying in bed. His leg hurt. His head was wrapped in bandages.

"Oh, Zoro," said Leonardo sadly, "it doesn't surprise me that Salai would disobey me. But *you*...

Perhaps I was wrong. Perhaps people will never fly. We are not birds. From now on I will stick to painting."

"No," said Zoro quietly. "Remember what you told me — one day people WILL fly! The machine was too heavy, that's all."

Leonardo thought for a moment. Then he jumped up.

"Yes!" he shouted. "And the wings should be longer. Like this…"

And he threw open his notebook and began to work,

slowly and patiently until a beautiful drawing appeared —

a *new* flying machine, more amazing than ever.

And while he worked, Leonardo began to smile;

a mysterious, gentle smile as if he could see far into the future

where boys and girls just like Zoro would sail through the clouds…

...and anything is possible.

LEONARDO DA VINCI

was born in 1452, the son of a rich lawyer and a poor peasant woman.

This great genius of the Italian Renaissance left few paintings, but his many notebooks give insight into a man who, according to the painter and biographer Vasari, was 'marvellously endowed by heaven with beauty, grace and talent in such abundance that he leaves other men far behind.' Vasari also notes that the gentle vegetarian was strong enough to bend a horseshoe with his bare hands.

Leonardo conceived the breathtaking plan of making a pictorial record of every object in the world. He was a supremely talented painter, architect, musician, military engineer, botanist, mathematician, astronomer and above all, inventor. Many of his devices were doomed to failure because of the limits of contemporary materials, but his designs for tanks, submarines, parachutes, hoists, pulleys and levers were uncannily ahead of their time and he became a favourite at the courts of Milan and France.

Leonardo's obsession with flight lasted throughout his life. It is unlikely that his contraptions stayed airborne for long, but he certainly made several attempts and Zoro's leap from Mount Ceccero became legendary. Zoro (Zoroaste de Peretolo) was one of Leonardo's many apprentice pupils as was 'Salai' Giacomo (1480-1524) who was taken in by Leonardo at ten years old. Leonardo recorded Salai's many thefts and delinquent acts, and at one point wrote the words, "THIEF, LIAR, OBSTINATE GLUTTON!" in the margin of his notebook, in which Salai later scribbled obscene drawings. The untalented and mischievous boy stayed with Leonardo until the master's death in 1519 and Leonardo even left him substantial property. Salai met a predictably reckless end when he was killed by a crossbow.

Zoro's history is less well documented but he undoubtedly became a highly talented artist who contributed to his master's great paintings, where their brush marks are now inseparable.

quando il vento ti sia dirieto alza l'alie

se l'alia da l'avanto fussi sotto vento
ha opposito e dirizassi a vn moto pure a
alla cossa lena sia mossa e bbliqua esta
e sicsi stia opposito

e se l'alia si pecto sara sopra vento abbass
ma se l'alia opposita laqual sia posta sotto vento
tata molto e dirizi a nocollo

ma se l'alia e la scena sara sotto ven
si ribbe alzare l'alia opposita e mostrar
si subito lanosi si dirizera

e se l'uccello sara dalla parte sinistra sopra
ra si ribbe mettere l'ala da sotto vento
si raggual gliara lo potere

quando l'uccello avrà le sue parti di vento
nto s'abbassera in ma colla costa
e si dirizera

MORE TITLES IN THE ANHOLT'S ARTISTS SERIES

CAMILLE AND THE SUNFLOWERS

"One day a strange man arrived in Camille's town. He had
a straw hat and a yellow beard…" The strange man is the artist Vincent van Gogh,
seen through the eyes of a young boy entranced by Vincent's painting.

ISBN 0-7112-2156-1

DEGAS AND THE LITTLE DANCER

Marie wanted to be the most famous ballerina in the world,
and when the artist Degas uses her as his model, her dream comes true.

ISBN 0-7112-2157-X

THE MAGICAL GARDEN OF CLAUDE MONET

When Julie crawls into a mysterious garden, she meets an old man tending the flowers.
The gentle gardener turns out to be the great artist, Claude Monet, and together
they explore his magical world. Monet and Julie wander across the Japanese bridge,
around the house and studios and they float through water gardens
where lilies sparkle as bright as stars.

ISBN 0-7112-2104-9

PICASSO AND THE GIRL WITH A PONYTAIL

Shy Sylvette is astonished when Pablo Picasso, the famous artist,
chooses her to be his model. As the pictures become larger and more extraordinary,
Picasso helps Sylvette to be brave and realise her dreams.

ISBN 0-7112-1177-9

**Frances Lincoln titles are available from all good bookshops.
You can also buy books and find out more about your favourite titles,
authors and illustrators on our website: www.franceslincoln.com.**